Written by
Timothy Knapman

Illustrated by
David Walker

D1434523

The GREAT EASTER EGG SCRAMBLE

It's Easter Bunny's party today
And all his friends are on their way,

He's made them cakes and buns and sweets,
Ice cream, fudge and chocolate treats!

To Alice, Jocelyn and Reuben,
with love – TK

Especially for Lucas
– DW

First published 2012 by Macmillan Children's Books, an imprint of Pan Macmillan, 20 New Wharf Road, London N1 9RR. Associated companies throughout the world. www.panmacmillan.com. ISBN: 978-1-5098-2674-2 Text copyright © Timothy Knapman 2012. Illustrations copyright © David Walker 2012. Moral rights asserted. All rights reserved. No part of this publication may be reproduced, stored in a retrieval system, or transmitted, in any form or by any means (electronic, mechanical, photocopying, recording or otherwise), without the prior written permission of the publisher. A CIP catalogue for this book is available from the British Library. Printed in China. 9 8 7 6 5 4 3 2 1

Look, swings and slides to play on too.

A merry-go-round – so much to do!

Then he lifts a cloth and sees, with a shiver . . .

. . . the basket of eggs he was meant to deliver!

He gets on his whizzy-wheeled, super-quick bike.
And scrambles off down the road, fast as you like!

"Brown is for Chicken, Duck's shell is blue.
The green egg is meant for Mrs Emu.

Crocodile's is yellow, Turtle's is white.
And the egg for the Penguins is cold – yes, that's right!"

Let's hope Easter Bunny won't scramble the rhyme.

"Brown is for Emu . . . Oh, look at the time!"

"Mrs Chicken!

I'm sorry I'm late," Bunny cries.

"Thanks for the egg," she says.

"My, what a size!"

She sits down to warm it: she knows what to do.

It hatches and out comes . . .

A BABY EMU!

But Bunny is off and he's reached Mrs Duck.

"You've brought me an egg Easter Bunny, what luck!"

But a duck egg's not yellow and big as a rock.

And when it cracks open . . .

Great snakes!

It's A CROC!

Now the Emus are happy. "An egg," they both sigh.
But their little house is all tidy and dry.

How will they feel when they find their new daughter's
A TURTLE who splashes the whole place with water?

Mrs Crocodile's sunning herself by the river,
When Bunny calls by with an egg to deliver.

It's blue and it's small, and was that a cluck?
What have you given her, Bunny?

A DUCK!

"The egg for the Turtles is cold – is that right?
Hot ones or cold ones, they're all a delight!"

But then the egg opens and – oh deary me!

Out strides . . .

. . . A PENGUIN, as proud as can be!

Quick! The last of the eggs is beginning to hatch . . .

And off Bunny rides. "I've a party to run!
Come along later, you're sure to have fun!"

Then the egg splits apart and the Penguins both shout,

As – WOW! – a poor frozen CHICKEN pops out!

So everyone's got the wrong baby,

Oh dear!

And no one's enjoying the party, that's clear.

It's up to Bunny to sort out this mess.

He says, "Onto the merry-go-round, children, yes!"

Now everyone's got the right baby . . .

. . . at last!